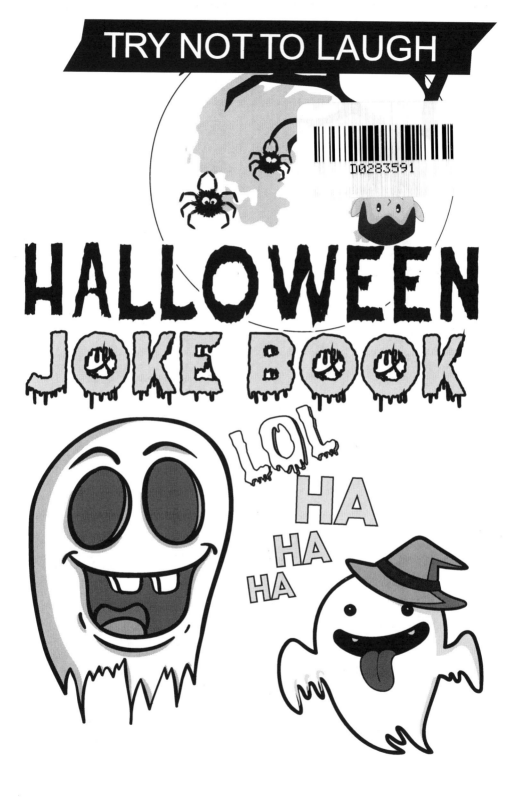

HALLOWEEN
JOKE BOOK

LOL
HA
HA
HA

D0283591

Halloween Challenge
Game Rules

Choose your team or do a one Vs one.

Face each other and make eye-contact.

Read jokes for each other by taking turns.

When your opponent laughs, you get a point.

You can make silly faces. If you laugh you lose.

Whoever wins more points at the end of the game, WINS.

Q: Why did the vampire read the newspaper?

A: He heard it had great circulation.

Q: How do vampires get around on Halloween?

A: On blood vessels.

Q: What do you call two witches living together?

A: Broommates.

Q: What position does a ghost play in hockey?

A: Ghoulie.

Q: What Halloween candy is never on time for the party?

A: Choco-LATE!

Q: What do witches put on to go trick or treating?

A: Mas-scare-a.

Q: Why don't skeletons ever go trick or treating?

A: Because they have no-body to go with.

Q: Why did the ghost starch his sheet?

A: He wanted everyone scared stiff.

Q: What do witches use on their hair?

A: Scare-spray

Q: What is in a ghost's nose?

A: Boo-gers.

Q: What was the witch's favorite subject in school?

A: Spelling

Q: What do you call two witches who live together?

A: Broom-mates!

Q: How do you fix a broken jack-o'-lantern?

A: With a pumpkin patch!

Q: What do witches ask for at a hotel?

A: Broom service.

Q: How does a scarecrow drink his juice?

A: With a straw!

Q: What did one ghost say to the other ghost?

A: Do you believe in people?

Q: How does a vampire enter his house?

A: Through the bat flap!

Q: Why do Jack-o-lanterns have wicked smiles?

A: Because they just had their brains scooped out!

Q: What happened to the man who didn't pay his exorcist?

A: The house was repossessed.

Q: What did the girl horse dress up as for Halloween?

A: A night mare.

Q: How do you fix a broken pumpkin?

A: A pumpkin patch.

Q: What do you get if you cross an exam with blood?

A: A blood test.

Q: Why did Dracula become a vegetarian?

A: He heard *stake* was bad for his heart.

Q: Why are there fences around cemeteries?

A: Because people are dying to get in.

Q: Who calls the shots at the Halloween party?

A: The gHost.

Q: What did the corpse's mom do when she got mad at him?

A: Grounded him.

Q: What happened to the cannibal who was late to dinner?

A: They gave him the cold shoulder.

Q: Who does a mummy take on a date?

A: Any old girl he can dig up.

Q: Why did the headless horseman go into business?

A: He wanted to get ahead in life.

Q: Why did the skeleton cross the road?

A: To get to the body shop.

Q: What's a phantom's favorite park ride?

A: The roller ghoster.

Q: Why wasn't there any food left after the monster party?

A: Because everyone was a-goblin.

Q: What happens when you goose a ghost?

A: You get a hand full of sheet.

Q: The maker of this product does not want it, the buyer does not use it, and the user does not see it. What is it?

A: A coffin.

Q: What's a ghoul's favourite bean?

A: A human bean.

Q: What's it called when a vampire has trouble with his house?

A: A grave problem.

Q: What would be the national holiday for a nation of vampires?

A: Fangs-giving!

Q: What do birds say on Halloween to get candy?

A: Twick-or-tweet

Q: What do you get if you divide the circumference of a jack-o-lantern by its diameter?

A: Pumpkin pi

Q: Why did the headless horseman go into business?

A: He wanted to get ahead in life.

Q: Where do werewolves store their junk?

A: A were-house.

Q: Where do ghosts like to go swimming?

A: Lake Erie.

Q: What did the werewolf eat after his teeth cleaning?

A: The dentist.

Q: Why was the ghost crying?

A: He wanted his mummy.

The skeleton played a melodic solo riff on his shiny sax-a-bone.

That skeleton sure brought his appetite to the picnic—and also some spare ribs.

Every Sunday, the skeleton plays his organ for the congregation.

Skeletons are great at stand-up comedy—when they use their funny bone.

There are two skeleton teachers at school. One is humerus, but the other is very sternum.

Q: Mummy, why do all the other kids call me a hairy werewolf?

A: Now stop talking about that and brush your face!

Q:What kind of fruit should you eat on Halloween?

A: A blood orange.

Q:How many abominable snow monsters does it take to screw in a lightbulb?

A: Only one, but you have to believe in it first.

Q: What did the trick-or-treater get when he told a hilarious joke?

A: Snickers

Q: Why did the werewolf go to the dressing room when she saw the full moon?

A: She needed to change.

Q: When does a ghost eat breakfast?

A: In the moaning.

Q: What sounds do witches make when they eat cereals?

A: Snap, CACKLE, and pop.

Q: Why did the kid dressed King Tut stop eating candy?

A: She had a mummy-ache.

Q: What do vampires fear the most?

A: Tooth decay

Made in the USA
Middletown, DE
05 October 2022